DON'T ASK, DON'T TELL
"YOU, ME, AND SHE"

S. L. DAVIS

Copyright © 2024 S. L. Davis

All rights reserved. This publication, or any part thereof, may not be reproduced in any form or by any means, including electronic, photographic, or mechanical, or by any sound recording system or by any device for storage and retrieval of information without the written permission of the copyright owner.

DEDICATION

This book is dedicated to all the men with a story to tell but are afraid to be heard… just know that I hear you loud and clear. To the women that have their back and never gave up on them ….I see you🌿

And above all things, have fervent love for one another, for "love will cover a multitude of sins."
1 Peter 4:8

TABLE OF CONTENTS

ALL THE WAY UP	5
TWO CAN PLAY THAT GAME	20
CUTE AND MUTE	22
CHARGE IT TO THE GAME	28
DON'T GET CAUGHT SLIPPIN	32
DECATUR WHERE IT'S GREATER	37
MIND THE BUSINESS THAT PAYS YOU	40
NEVER BITE THE HAND THAT FEEDS YOU	45
CANDYMAN	49
RUSSIAN ROULETTE	53
PUT ME IN THE GAME COACH	57
SAVE ME FROM MYSELF	63
ALL ISN'T FAIR IN LOVE AND WAR	71

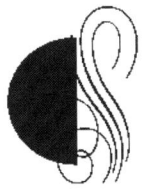

ALL THE WAY UP

🎵🎵*Do you know what today is? It's our Anniversary* 🎵🎵, I sang as I grabbed Deasha, also known as "Dee," from behind while looking at us both in the mirror. "Look at my lil trap queen…looking all good and shit!!!" I said. "I don't know why they scheduled this board during our anniversary, but I guess first things first," said Dee, as she loosened my grip from her hips to turn around to straighten up the button on my shirt. "Why are you so nervous? It's not like you haven't gone before the board before," she said. "Hell, I know that baby, but this step up could possibly change our lives. You remember always saying you wanted a house in our names, right? I mean, staying in this apartment is all well and good, but this will definitely be a game changer and get us to the 'Promised Land,'" I said as I laughed. "Plus, we can pay off the debt from your foreclosure sooner, and CSM Bates told me that if... I mean, when I get promoted, this will put me over 3rd platoon". "I believe in you, bae," said Dee. "You got this!!!!" she said as she slapped me on the ass. "You think I can get a little ummm?" I said as I nudged her. "Hell no!!!!" she said. "OK, well, wish me luck," I said as I grabbed a half-eaten bagel from the kitchen table. "Luck, you don't need no stinkin' luck when you have God on your side baby...remember that!!!" she said as she closed the door.

***

Going over these flashcards I've been studying for the upcoming promotion really messed me up. I mean, I can't remember shit. How am I supposed to stand up straight, remember this, recite that?! I should just turn around and say FUCK THIS! At least in the streets, I never had to stress over no damn board. Dodge a couple of bullets, maybe but not stress over a damn promotion board. Did I study all this time for nothing? I was popping these answers off left and right when SSG Wallace stood before me doing a mock board. Now look at my ass, shining shoes, creasing pants, and shit. I sure could use a blunt right now.

"You ready?" asked MSG Washington as I walked in the door. I said. "Yes, Master Sergeant," but I really meant to say, "Hell No, I ain't about to stand here and let these people who don't know my life judge me and tell me if I am or am not capable of doing my job." I still have time to back out. "You up next, Smith," MSG Washington said as she walked him into the boardroom. "SGT Smith present..I mean reporting". Damn, I messed up already. I was shaking like a $2 stripper. I told myself, get yourself together because Dee and the kids depend on you.

I stood there trembling for what felt like hours. The questions were thrown left and right, and my palms were sweating profusely. "You good?" asked CSM White. I must have looked like I was about to pass out, but I responded, "I'm good, CSM.". "OK, we can carry on," he said. They then asked me to sing the damn Army Song... the damn Army Song, of all things. I got this, I said to myself. I started marching in a place like I was told to do in the mock board and began to belch out what I thought was the Army song but halfway through, I got a complete brain fart. God, please be with me. All I keep hearing in my head is R. Kelly singing 🎵You remind me of my Jeep🎵. If I don't get my shit together, I'm gonna be reminded of what the streets look like.

Suddenly, my memory returned, and I was spitting the answers out left and right. This is what I'm talking about; I'm on a muthaf**kin roll. I just can't let my baby down. She's been through so much, and I vowed to be there for her and the kids for better or worse. On top of all that, we have a newborn. I don't know about anyone else, but I'm all the way up right now. I feel blessed, and I got this board in the bag minus a few hiccups.

"How do you think you did, my boi?" SSG Green asked as he patted me on the back. I scurried to open the office door to escape all the stress I just encountered. "Damn, can I get in the office first before you bombard me with 21 Questions, 50 cents?!" I said jokingly. "Oh, I'm sorry, my boi, but seriously, how do you think you did?" Asked Green again. I never said anything; I just looked at him and shook my head. Taj Green is my best friend and partner in crime. We both came from the hard streets of Atlanta. I grew up in Decatur, and he grew up on the Southside, and we got it out of the mud together.

Now, we are just trying to make a better life for our families. No one taught us a damn thing about leaving a legacy for our kids and our kids' kids. What we were taught was that robbing Peter to pay Paul was OK. I guess that's why I sucked at word problems in school. I mean, if Peter had 5 kilos of cocaine and I bought 2 kilos, how much does Peter have in total? The answer is zero because Peter ain't got shit. I'm gonna take everything he got, and that's on Gawd. It's just that simple, and Green and I think alike. The only issue is that Green never really let go of the streets. He always told me that if I needed anything, I could definitely get back in the game, and he showed me how easy it was to flip a brick and transport "SNOW" in a GSA (Government Service Administration) vehicle. He is definitely a wild boi.

I remember riding with him during lunch one day to a local McDonald's near the base. I thought we would pick up something to eat and head back, but when we pulled up to the building, there was a black E550 Mercedes with black tinted windows, parked behind us, somewhat blocking us in. My anxiety immediately kicked in. This was unusual; I mean, there were several vacant parking spaces, so why were they parked behind us? What happened next gave me pause. Green gave me his money and told me to go inside and order him a #1 with no cheese. I said OK, but as I walked towards the building, I saw my boi jump out of the vehicle with his black backpack in one hand as he headed over to the black Mercedes. I could tell by the way he moved that something was shifty and intentional about this meetup.

This shit was already planned, and the way he insisted on McDonald's instead of the Church's Chicken, which was right before you got to the McDonald's, was a little odd, to say the least. You know they say black folks love some damn chicken. It was only odd because we ate at Church's Chicken every Tuesday. It's the only place you could get a 3-piece dinner for $2.99 and still have money left over for a blunt. Can you say "Winning"?! Needless to say, he and a tall, slender guy dressed in an MCM designer tracksuit stood behind the car and began to exchange whatever was in the bag. I was so fixated on what was going on outside that I damn near missed placing my order. "Can I help you??? I SAID, CAN I HELP YOU???" screamed the lady with red, green, and yellow braids behind the counter as she scrolled through her phone. "Oh, yeah. Can I get a #1? Hold the cheese with a medium sprite." I tried not to look back out the window, but I couldn't help it.

"Is that all, sir??? Helllooo!!! IS THAT ALL, SIR???" shouted the lady. "Oh, my bad. Can I also get a #2C without cheese?" I just know this niggah aint back to his old tricks and pulling some foul shit.

While waiting for my order, I noticed the Mercedes was gone, and Green was back in the GSA. I can't wait to find out who that was. After retrieving my order and returning to the vehicle, I noticed a distinctive smell in the air. It smelled like Reggie, which is another name for regular weed. It wasn't grown in a lab but in the backyard. "Aye, man, who the hell was that?" I asked as I got in the van "... and I hope yo ass ain't been smoking in this van, man!!!!" "You can smell it?!" he asked. "Umm, hell yeah, I can, and you better not get me in trouble. You know I'm trying to stay clean so I can get promoted. Don't fuck up what I have because you can't get yo shit right." "Man, we're good...I promise, plus I got this blunt spray. Here, smell it (as he pushes it in my face). Shit smells good, ain't it?! Pina Colada Mango!!!!" "This shit hit hard as fuck!!!!" he uttered. "Whatever, man, like I said, don't get me in trouble."

At that point, I didn't even care who it was; I was just trying to keep my nose clean. Four years prior, I was almost sent to jail for being in the wrong place at the wrong time, and they flagged me in the system, which prohibited me from getting promoted by fooling with Taj's ass. I really aint trying to fuck this up. Friend or no friend, I'm not trying to lose my lady over no stupid shit. Speaking of my lady, I need to leave this office to celebrate my Anniversary. I'll worry about the results of the board later on.

***

After work, I couldn't get home quickly enough. As soon as I walked in the door, I could smell the sweet aroma of Jo Malone's Cardamom and Mimosa mixed with the scent of a well-seasoned steak. Taj's girlfriend, Tasha, who happens to be close to my wife, Dee, and I picked up the kids to give us a break for the night. She's such a sweetheart, but I'm sure Taj will also sabotage this relationship like any other female he's been with. Taj better not bring his ass over here today, knowing I barely get a chance to spend with wifey, and we need all the quality time we can get. Being a stepfather is demanding, but their fathers do a great job stepping in. I didn't have that when I was growing up (A strong father figure, that is). The streets raised me, so I guess that's why I keep Taj around. He's my brother, although aggravating, he's my brother nonetheless.

"Hey baby, is that you?!" Called a sweet voice from the far end of the apartment. I walked to the back, greeted with nothing but a smile. "Damn baby, this was not what I was expecting. I guess we better make the most of our time," I said. "Before we go any further, let me start by saying that these past 2 years have been the best I have ever had in my life, and this would have never happened if I hadn't lost my ID card. There you were, looking good as hell. Waiting in line. I knew you wanted me by the way you kept staring at me," I said as I laughed. "Umm, no, I was wondering why your hairline was so far back," Dee said, pushing me on my shoulder while giggling. "You got jokes," I said. "No, being honest, I didn't think I would ever get married because of my past lifestyle, and you gave me such a hard time trying to get to know you, and for good reason, I am aware of, but it just made me feel I was destined to be alone," I said. "I'm sorry, baby," said Dee. "I'm just glad God sent you in at the right time. Enough about that because I don't want you to start crying," Dee jokingly said. "Now come here and give me some lovin'."

"Hold up, let me jump in the shower and wash up unless you want some of this promotion board dick," I said as I laughed and took off my clothes, throwing them on the floor in the corner. "Don't get slapped on our anniversary," said Dee as she picked his uniform up off the floor and placed it in the basket next to the door in the bathroom. 🎵 There's a meeting in my bedroom 🎵 was playing in the background. She just couldn't wait until I got out, so she opened the shower curtain to get the party popping early.

13

She slowly crept in behind me and started kissing on my back. "Damn, so this is how you gonna do me?!" I said as I slowly turned around and began kissing her on her shoulder. Her hair was pulled back in a loose ponytail that hung to the nape of her neck. It was slightly damp from the previous shower she had taken just before I came home, but if she didn't mind getting it wet again, I was happy to oblige. I started caressing her small but perky breast as she threw her head back to avoid the water hitting her in the face. She opened her eyes slightly and tilted her head just enough to watch me devour her body. "Don't stop, baby," she said as she grabbed the back of my head. It was something about the way she grabbed the back of my head; it made me feel that safe and wanted. I lifted her from the shower and took her back to the bedroom. As I prepared to lay her down, she grabbed me around my neck to secure her position. Once I began to enter her, our eyes connected with every stroke. Back in the day, I would dare look into the eyes of a female I was casually beating down, and I most definitely wouldn't fuck her from the front. This creates feelings. Have you ever seen a dog fuck another dog from the front… just won't happen. But not her; she's my lady, my baby, and my world. I have to connect our souls.

I slowly removed myself from her pulsating walls, turned her on her stomach, and kissed the nape of her neck until I reached the crease of her ass, which sat up like two melons. I took both of my hands and spread her legs apart like I was parting the Red Sea. As she tightly gripped the pillow placed beneath her, I told her to arch her back. I began to lick from the open hole of never-ending waterfalls to the pearl that sat above it. She always loved that position. I let my tongue glide back and forth until my tongue became numb, and she couldn't take it anymore. "Can I turn back over, baby, so that I can see you going in and out of me?" asked Dee as she slowly turned over while still trying to hold herself steady. I then began stroking faster and faster until we both climaxed. "You're the only man I've ever been comfortable enough to allow myself to be free with," she said. "You don't have to worry about that from this point on; I promise I got you. Now, go in there and make me a plate, woman," I said as we both peeled ourselves from the soaked sheets.

"What's on the agenda for today, baby?" I asked as I approached the kitchen, trying to tie up my pajama pants. "I mean, we don't have the kids for tonight (I slapped her on the ass as I sat down to eat) which is hardly ever, and we can just relax." "Nothing much, babe, but since we are free, I have some things I want to talk to you about," Dee said. "What's up?" I said with a look of concern on my face. She placed the plate before me and kissed me on the forehead. "You know I love you, right?" she said as if trying to convince herself. "But," "Oh Lawd, when you say "BUT," it's always something concerning," I exclaimed while trying to scarf down the meal she had just placed before me. "No, I was just going to say maybe you should scale back from hanging around Taj, and when I say scale, I mean move all the way back from him. Tasha was telling me, he seems to be dibbling back and forth in the game".

I personally knew he never stopped but assumed that he learned his lesson and slowed down, but I couldn't tell her that. If she really knew, she would flip her fucking wig and peel my muffin cap back blue…lol. OK, this is not a laughing matter, I thought to myself. I allowed her to ramble on and on about how he wasn't the company I needed. She continued on, saying, "I thought he learned his lesson from the last time, but from what I see, if he keeps playing with fire, he is going to lose the best thing he has going for him, which is Tasha. She didn't know that we had made a pact to never leave one another's side despite the mess he had placed himself in. He was my family, and Dee is just going to have to deal with it, one way or another. He was there before her and will be there when she's not around.

"Can we table this conversation, Dee? Because every time we start talking about Taj, it throws a wedge in what we are trying to build. I told you that I think he's a changed man," I said as I got up from the table, raising my voice so she could know how serious I was about this conversation. My temperament was one not to be challenged, but neither was hers. "I mean damn, I can't be with him 24 hrs a day, 7 days a week, so I'm going to take his word for it. I don't even feel like eating now," I said as I pushed back from the table, leaving only a corner of food on the plate. "What the hell are you getting upset about?" Dee said. "You act like you owe him your life." "Well, I kinda do," I said, turning around and shouting from the hallway. "You really know how to fuck up a good evening, don't you?!" A tear fell from her eyes, but she refused to let me hear her cry. I wasn't going to get the best of her today. Dee knew what battles to pick so she just turned around and started washing dishes "I'm kid-free, and if he wants to pout, he can do it alone, she thought to herself. I just don't understand why in the hell he always allows Taj to drag him (us) into shit. I'm done thinking about it. Let me just finish cleaning this place up and take my ass to bed. We could have kept the kids for this shit."

***

(Ding Dong) It's 4:00 a.m. Now, who in the hell could possibly be at someone's door at this time of morning? I thought to myself as I rolled over, trying to wipe the crust out of my eye while looking over to the right side of the bed to make sure Dee was lying there, but she wasn't. As I approached the living room, I realized that she never came to bed; she was sprawled out on the couch with one leg on the couch and the other on the floor dangling. Next to her was a partially drunk glass of Dublin wine that she strategically laid next to her laptop. I should kick it over onto the computer and tell her ass she did it, but I ain't that nasty. "Who is it?" I said as I approached the door. Looking through the peephole, I could see a tall, slender man standing midway between the steps and the porch as if he was confused about the apartment he had just wandered up to but wanted to walk away. He looked like the guy I saw a while back at McDonald's, but why is he at my door this morning?

I unlocked the case sitting on the coffee table, grabbed my Glock, and returned to the door, but he was gone by the time I came back. What the fuck is going on? I looked back, and of course, Dee didn't move. I immediately texted Taj and asked him if he had sent someone by my house, but he didn't respond, so when Tasha dropped the kids off a few hours later, I asked her what Taj was up to. I could see Dee rolling her eyes out of my peripheral, so I kept the conversation to a minimum. Tasha then rolled her eyes and said, "He had duty last night, so I assume he's OK. I don't know why Washington always rides him." I'm thinking, "What duty?!" Taj didn't have duty last night, but I can't say anything because Inspector Gadget will be all over the case. I just replied with, "Oh, OK". This explains why he didn't answer my text with his trifling ass, but what's new.

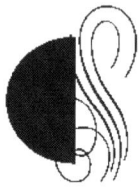

TWO CAN PLAY THAT GAME

"Can I talk to you outside, Dee?" asked Tasha. They both walked outside and left me inside with the kids. This was to make sure that I didn't eavesdrop. As soon as I walked close to the door to get a better listen, the door opened back up. "Oh, I forgot to tell you that you all are running out of milk," Tasha said, then closed the door abruptly before I could ask if everything was OK. She then sat on the steps while Dee stood with her back against the door. "What's up, girl?!" asked Dee. "Girl, Taj got me all the way fucked up! Did you know he lied about working last night? I found out because he left his phone on the counter unlocked, might I add? I wasn't going to look, but he's been moving differently lately. Anyway, the text said he had a drop off in Augusta, GA, close to some base called Fort Eisenhower, and a "PICK UP" on the way back to Fort Gillem. I know I'm wrong for looking, but all this extra duty he's claiming to have is going to catch up to his ass soon."

Dee then moved from the door and sat next to her. "I heard someone ring the doorbell in the wee hours of the morning, but I thought I was dreaming. I saw Jac walk towards the door, so I pretended to be asleep. He never opened the door, but I did see him grab his gun and ask who it was, but no one answered. I assumed it was the wrong house, and he never said anything to me this morning. I wonder if it had anything to do with Taj's ass? It will be a matter of time before whatever is going on will come to a head, but for now, I'm going to keep it cute and mute." They shook their heads in disbelief, got up from the steps, and said their goodbyes. Then, Tasha went on her way.

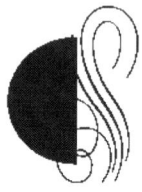

CUTE AND MUTE

"What's up with Tasha? She seemed annoyed," I said as I handed her the baby. "Oh, nothing, family issues," she replied. "Oh, OK," I replied. "I know you're not supposed to keep secrets from your spouse, but if he didn't say anything about that 4:00 a.m. visit, I won't say anything either." "You see, trust has never been my strong point. I thought we were a team, but it seems as if he wants to be an OP." I grabbed my keys and slowly walked towards the door. "Well, I'm about to meet up with some of the boys unless you have something else in mind," I said as I twirled the key ring on my index finger. "Damn, this niggah always got someplace to go when I need him. I swear I feel like a single parent all over again at times. He must not know who the fuck I am. He better be glad God got a hold of me before he did, and don't think because I said God right after I cursed means that I don't have him in me. It's niggahs that bring the old Dee out," Dee thought.

***

As I approached the car, I gave Taj a call to find out what is going on. (*RIIINNNGGG…RIIINNNGGG!!!!*) "Man, where are you? You know what, never mind that… did you send someone by my home the other day, like 4:00 a.m.?" "Hell no!! Why?!" Taj replied. "It looked like the same dude I saw you with…never mind, man (because I know he was about to lie)." At this point, I know he's going to act like he has amnesia. "The better question is, why did you lie about having duty?" I asked. "Yo, meet me off Peachtree at the Old Rio Bell Grande," Taj requested. "Why?! What's going on out there?" I asked. "I gotta straighten some things out, and I need your help." I wanted to tell his ass, "No," but I knew if I needed him, he would be there, no questions asked.

I pulled up as he requested, and to my surprise (maybe not my surprise because, after all, it's Taj we are talking about). His ass is nowhere in sight. Let me call and see where this niggah is. (*RIIINNNGGG…RIIINNNGGG!!!!*) "YO!"

answered Taj from the other end. "Where the hell are you? I just left my house, and Deeasha is in her feelings today, so I'm not up for your shit," I advised him. "Man, I'm here. Look over to your left. I'm in the gray Honda Accord next to the white van," he said. "OK," I replied, "But who is that next to you?" I asked. "Man, that's an ole girl from the unit, Butler. She hangs out with Robinson in Echo Company," Taj replied. "OOOOK, so why am I here?!" I said, seemingly miffed. "Well, she….and don't say nothing, just listen…she just had an abortion (he whispered softly), and I knew that if I told you where I was and why I needed you, you might not have come". "You damn right!!" I said. "Why am I here, man? Spill it," I said as he began to get upset. "I need you to take her to Robinson's barracks. I gotta get home. I've been gone since yesterday, and I think Tasha might be suspecting something," he said as he lowered his voice. "No shit Sherlock," I said as I hung up the phone. Now, I see why he said I should meet him at the damn Rio Bell Grande. It's ironically across from Planned Parenthood, an abortion clinic located dead in the heart of Atlanta. I could have sworn Butler was married to ole boy from our Battalion who just went overseas a few months back, but that's not my business. "Just don't get me caught up in this mess, is all I ask."

He walked his linky ass over and placed her in my backseat, like I agreed to this. I can tell she was ashamed, or at least I thought she should be if it's not her husband's baby, but I digress. I gave him the look of death as he closed the door, trying not to look in my direction, placing me once again in the middle of his shit. "I must have a hunger for punishment or just a damn fool," I said to myself. Taj immediately walked away, tapped the hood of my car as to say, "I'm out," and threw up the deuces, jumped in the Honda, and drove off into the Sunset or back home to pretend he had duty. Here I am, trying to make small talk with someone I barely even speak to. Her mouth is ruthless, and her attitude matches her mouth. From what I heard, she was full of drama. "Which barracks am I taking you to Butler?" I asked sternly so she didn't get confused about my position in this. "I'm just a voluntold Uber driver," I thought to myself as she laid in the fetal position in the back seat. She mumbled softly, "McGriff." "Ok," I replied, placing the directions in my GPS and turning my music on low. This niggah owes me an explanation on so much.

You see, Taj grew up always doing the most, even when he didn't have to. I remember back in middle school, we would go to the candy shop, and while everyone else was buying Laffy Taffys, Now and Laters, or Jingles, he was buying candy cigarettes and drinking root beer. He did the absolute most as a kid, but to us, he was the man. Honestly, Taj had more opportunities than the rest of us, although we were both raised in the hood. Throughout high school, he was one of the most sought-after athletes. This fool even had a scholarship to Georgia State… GEORGIA FUCKING STATE, but messed that up by getting caught up on Flat Shoals selling weight. That's when they told him he could either join the military or go to jail. "I'll take the military for $200, Alex," Taj exclaimed!!! That's when I decided that the Army also didn't sound so bad.

I could definitely use a change of pace from the scenery around here. I used to stay at Taj's house most of the time because although his father wasn't a part of his life, his mom stepped in and attended all the games, kept food on the table, and made sure he kept his ass in school. Where we're from, that's unheard of. Most of the time, the parents were so cracked out or in prison that they only had time to worry about themselves. He chose the life he wanted to be a part of. I, on the other hand, had no one. My mom got locked up when I was 6 after being convicted of a burglary in the first degree, which made it a felony, and was sentenced to 7 years behind bars, but because she couldn't get her shit together while imprisoned, she found herself once again in trouble. She stabbed a correctional officer and was given life without parole.

I must not have meant that much to her because she never thought about me or what would happen to my little sister and me when she wasn't around. This is where my distrust for women developed. My pops died of AIDS shortly after getting out of prison, and I, of course, was tossed to and fro in the foster system until my aunt took me and my little sister in. Unfortunately, my little sister was killed in a drive-by less than three weeks after my dad passed while playing outside on the porch. You can say that the odds were definitely stacked against me in life. Ms. Green, Taj's mother, was my lifesaver when it came to ensuring I was at every football practice. She and my aunt became close enough for me to spend most nights with them. My aunt really didn't believe in spending the night with anyone. She was afraid I would be molested or taken advantage of. Only God knows why she took a third-shift job.

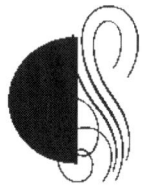

CHARGE IT TO THE GAME

I'm low key pissed, but I didn't want to make it more than what it was. This is damn sholl placing me in an awkward position. One, as I stated, I don't really know or like this girl. Two, she's married to another soldier. I wonder whether this was their baby or Taj moved in as soon as the coast was clear. I'm trying to get promoted, so I don't want to be tied up with her. Let me get her ass back to wherever she's going quickly. As soon as we pulled up, I saw Harris, one of my soldiers, ole talking ass dressed in her PT uniform, sitting on the curb, on the phone. She was the roving reporter for the military and always running her mouth. All she did was talk about what Facebook said and what TikTok showed. If the military had a MOS for

TikTokers, she would definitely qualify. Now, how in the hell am I supposed to get this girl out of my vehicle without looking like we have something going on?! Man, this has to be the worst day of my life, or is it?

Robinson, the soldier I was dropping Butler off to, was walking down the steps, so I assumed she got the memo and knew what was going on. She stopped and chopped it up with Harris about God knows what as she walked her slow-acting ass over to my car. "What you got going on, big Sarg?!" she asked as she stood with her nose pressed against my window. Ugh, she makes me sick. I swear I hate being placed in uncomfortable situations. "Nothing, I'm just dropping her off. Can you please get her out of my car?" I said. I wanted to get the hell out of here as quickly as possible. "Yo, Butler, wake yo ass up," I said as I turned around to her while she was lying in the backseat. Robinson leaned into the car and proceeded to shake her, but she was unresponsive. Damn, I don't want to have to get out of the car; this was supposed to be an easy transaction. "Aye, man, don't play like that," I said frantically. "I'm not playing, she's not waking up, and there is blood all over your backseat," Robinson said. "What the fuck do you mean she ain't responding?! "I'm about to put her ass out right here, and y'all figure that shit out." At this point, I'm getting pissed off. I can not be in any mess. I'm trying to get promoted, and Dee will kill me even if this has nothing to do with me. The scenario will not play out well.

I tried to get Taj ass on the phone and to no avail. He always turns his phone off after doing some fuck shit. This is his problem, not mine. Now, what am I supposed to do? I jumped in the back seat through the front; mind you, nosey ass Harris was still on the phone, sitting outside. This will definitely give her something to gossip about. I damn near felt like Ike Turner when he told Tina, "If you don't make it, I'll kill you bitch." I didn't know which hat to put on... NCO of the Army or NCO of the streets. Old me would have left her ass here, but I can't have this on my conscience in case there is something seriously wrong with her. "Butler..Butler," I called as I damn near shook her shoulder off. She wasn't waking up, and blood was pouring out. I told Robinson that we have to come up with a plan without Harris seeing us. We decided that I would drive around to the back of the Barracks so she could open the back door to assist me with getting her into the building. At this point, blood is everywhere in my backseat. Robinson grabbed one arm, and I held the other. We proceeded to pull her from the car and carry her up to Robinson's room on the first floor. I pray to God that no one sees us, but what's the worst that can happen after this fiasco?

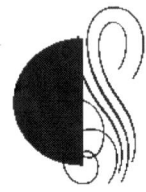

DON'T GET CAUGHT SLIPPIN

(RIIINNNGGG...RIIINNNGGG) "Where in the hell are you?" asked a frantic female voice from the other end. "I...I … I'm in the middle of trying to take care of some business for one of my soldiers". Now, I really didn't lie, but what doesn't have to be said will not have to be explained later on in court, ya feel me?! "Sounds sneaky to me, but anywho, I need you to pick up some diapers and milk from the store since you can't seem to bring your ass home and haven't reached out to me since you left. I assumed you were in a mood," said an exhausted Dee. "I told you I went to meet up with the boys, but then I had a short suspense. I'll be there shortly…promise," I said as I cracked the door open to look at the lifeless body lying prostrate on the floor.

Let me call this niggah again because this is not my problem, and it has trouble written all over it.

(*RIIINNNGGG…RIIINNNGGG!!!!*) He didn't answer, so I decided to leave a voicemail." HEY MAN, THIS IS NOT MY ISSUE AND IT HAS TURNED INTO SOME OTHER SHIT." (*BEEP!!!!*) Now he wants to call. This niggah, I thought to myself.... "What up, Jay Peezy?" Taj said as if this was a casual day. "Man, what the fuck?! This girl is bleeding, and it has gotten worse. Come take care of yo shit; I'm leaving". "Man, that girl is married; that ain't my issue, plus I can't leave because Tasha got the truck. I dropped the car back off to the rental place. Is she breathing? "What does that have to do with anything? Plus, this is your fucking issue, man.... I'm out. "I grabbed my keys out of my pocket and proceeded to leave the barracks. They will have to figure this shit out on their own. This wasn't the best decision, but honestly, what other choice did I have?! I'm trying to get promoted, and once again, here I go, being a fool for Taj. I don't understand for the life of me why I continue to put myself through this. (I cranked up my car and proceed to drive off).

I need a fucking drink after all of this. I prayed all was well with her, but that's all I could offer, I said as I grabbed the cross attached to my necklace and kissed it.

(*RIIINNNGGG…RIIINNNGGG!!!!*) "Hello" "Don't forget to go by the store," said Dee annoyingly. "I didn't forget. Hell, it was only 30 min ago that you asked me to, sheesh," I said as I hung up the phone. Now, I knew how much she hated being hung up on, but at this rate, it is what it is. (*RIIINNNGGG…RIIINNNGGG!!!!*) "Damn, what now," I thought to myself. "Hey, try that shit with someone else. You must be acting out for that new bitch" (*CLICK!!!!*). It seems like hanging up is the best thing to do. I really don't have time for this shit…I got Taj's ignorant ass, a possible dead woman, and aggravating ass Dee to deal with….really fuck my life!!!!

***

Pulling up to my house, I knew I was about to deal with some ish, but surprisingly, it was super mellow and chill. I opened the door and laid the items on the table, and instead of getting met with a fist, I got met with a kiss. Weird much, I thought to myself. She must be waiting to kill me in my sleep, which honestly, at this point, doesn't sound too bad. "You ate yet," Asked a calm but concerned

Dee. "Yep, I'm full," I answered back, knowing I was hungry as hell. Shit, she wasn't about to kill me. "The kids are asleep. Do you want to fool around?" she asked as she placed her hand down my pants. "I'm no fool; I ain't eating shit from her, but I'll take a slice of ass to go," I said to myself. "Umm OK…I guess if that's what you want to do, we can," I said shyly.

"Come in the laundry room," she said as she lifted her denim mini-skirt and dropped to her knees. Now, Dee wasn't a stranger to having sex in the laundry room; she performed her best work there. "Hurry up before the kids wake up, fool," she said as she pulled me closer. I didn't know that while she was down there, she was doing a scratch and sniff test to see if I was with someone else. At this point, that was the least of her worries. She began to suck on my flaccid dick until it became as erect as a shooting bullet. She loved how she took me from 87 to 93 in no time. This was one of the things I loved about her: her spontaneity. She could be on the verge of a meltdown and still want to get it poppin'. I don't know if this was love or her ass was crazy as hell. Either way, I'll take it.

I picked her up off the floor and sat her on top of the dryer next to the door. I turned the dryer on to somewhat disguise the mellifluous sounds about to be heard. As I rubbed the head of my penis against her clitoris, I could feel her ocean overflow, which excited me to move closer to the well in which her waters drifted heavily. As I entered her, I could feel her walls start to close in a while, massaging my hard dick, but just as I was about to climax, there was a knock at the door. "Momma, you OK?" asked a sweet and somewhat innocent voice from the other side of the door. "She's OK, go lay back down," I answered back. It would be perfect if that was the case, but not for us. They would just stand there until the door opened, looking crazy as hell. "I think we need to stop," said Dee. This was the story of our lives: start…then stop. "Man, we can't catch a break," I said as we pulled ourselves together. These blue balls were becoming a frequent thing for me, so much to the point that I almost expected this. My question is, what is she up to?

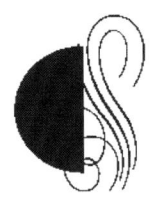

DECATUR WHERE IT'S GREATER

(*DING DONG!!!!*) "Who's at the door now?" I asked as I slowly walked to the door, still trying to zip up my pants. "Who is it?" I asked with concern in my voice. I looked out the door and noticed the po po was outside. "It's the Decatur Police Department," said the scraggly-looking officer standing between my storm door. Why are they on post? They are definitely out of their jurisdiction. "THE DECATUR POLICE DEPARTMENT?!" I repeated aloud as I cracked the door. "How may I help you?" I asked. "Is there a Tajohn Green here?" "Ummm, no one with that name stays here," I answered back with hesitance in my voice. "This is 3281 Hill Dr, right?!" asked the officer. "Yeah, it is, but no one by that name stays here. The officer gave me a stern look and walked away, but as he turned his back, I looked out the door, and there were two men sitting in the back of his car. What in the hell has this fool gotten himself into? It's like he's a glutton for punishment. Now, I'm gonna have to act like I am clueless to this shit.

"What did they want?" asked nosey ass Dee. "I think they had the wrong house, baby. They confused us with 3821, I believe." knowing I was lying. "Oh, OK, that's odd. Most of the time, their asses are on point. They're slackin'," said Dee as she picked the baby up off the floor and walked towards the back of the room. She immediately picked up the phone to call Tasha.

(*RIIINNNGGG…RIIINNNGGG!!!!*) "Hey girl, what the fuck is going on? I just heard the police at the door, and Jac said it was the wrong apartment, but I clearly heard them say Tajohn Green." "Are you serious?!" Tasha said as she whispered to me over the phone. "Taj is asleep right now, but give me a few to go through his shit." Hours passed, and no phone call came through from Tasha. Dee was waiting on edge to hear all the fucked up shit that he may have gotten himself into. It wouldn't be the first time, but who's counting? "Let me continue to clean up this mess these kids made and take my ass to bed," Dee said as she kicked the pile of toys out of her pathway.

Meanwhile, I was plotting a way to get out of the house. "Dee, where is my shaving cream?! I want to look fresh when I go to work. Being that I just went before the board." I knew she hated it when I asked her about things I only knew I needed. "I don't know, baby, check the cabinet by the toilet," she shouted from the back room. Hell, I knew I was low two days ago, but this will give me enough time to leave the house. "Damn, I'm low," I said, hoping she wouldn't say anything. I'll be back. Let me run to Walmart before it gets too late and pick some up," I said as I picked up my keys, nearly knocking the table over.

As soon as I walked out, I received a call from Robinson, who happened to be with nosey ass Harris, stating that she was at the hospital with Butler, who is now in intensive care, and they are trying to contact her husband through the Red Cross. "Do you know how to contact his commander?" she asked frantically. "Naw, but I'll try to see if I can find some info on him." Meanwhile, Taj's ass seems to be getting off scot-free.

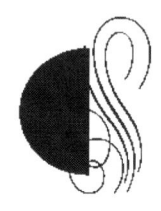

MIND THE BUSINESS THAT PAYS YOU

(*Cranks car*) ♪♪ *Your love is like a roller coaster. You make me wanna say it's over*♪♪ was playing on the radio. Let me change this station. (*flips station again*) ♪♪*This shit sounds like Black Boots, Jodeci grindin'*♪♪ "Man, I love listening to EQUE and Metal Roze, but I ain't in the mood for no lovey-dovey, making love shit," I said as I flipped through the stations once more. ♪♪*So, I'm outside of the club, and you think I'm a punk*♪♪. "That's more like it." 107.9 always gets the party poppin'," I said as I turned the block. Let me call Robinson to see what's going on with Butler.

(RIIINNNGGG…RIIINNNGGG!!!!) "Hey, Sarge, what's up? Any info?!" asked Robinson. "I was calling to see if you had any myself," I replied. "Oh no, but I did overhear someone say she was messing with a sergeant from our unit, but they got quiet when they noticed that I was there," she said while also answering questions being thrown at her from the other end. I'm so sorry that I had to bring Harris along, but she stopped by my room right after you left, and I had no one to turn to.

"You know this will be all over the place, right?!" I said. "I'm glad this doesn't have shit to do with me," I thought. "Aye, Sarge, hold on for a minute, that's Miss Bell, the Unit Administrator from his company, calling me," said Robinson. ('I waited for three minutes and then hung up). Let me call Taj ass again.

(RIIINNNGGG…RIIINNNGGG!!!!) "Yo!" answered Taj, sounding as though he had gotten a full night's rest and wasn't worried about shit. "Hey, do you know the ole girl is in intensive care, and they sent a Red Cross message to get her husband to come home, right?!" I said. "OK! Soooo, what does that have to do with me? Man, look, I'm sorry that shit happened to her, but umm, she's for the team. That can be anyone's baby," said an unbothered Taj. "I just," I interrupted. "You just what?! Want to mind yo' business?! Is that what you want to do?" Taj said as if I interrupted his day. "Man Fuck you," I said. (*BEEP!!!!*). "Man, hold on, that's Robinson calling about yo shit." "Well, answer 'cause it ain't. I decided to click over in the middle of Taj rambling.

"Hello, what's up?" "Update....she passed away, Big Sarge....she fucking passed away, man," said Robinson as she cried her bleeding heart out over the phone. "You sure?! Stop playing," I said frantically. "Yes, she was pronounced dead about an hour ago. Her husband is en route. The crazy part is there is talk of her being pregnant through hearsay". "Damn, you still don't miss a beat," I said. Thinking to myself, this is a nosey-ass girl. "I'll call you back. Someone is on the other line." I forgot that Taj was on hold. "OK. I'll keep you posted," she said. "Don't tell anyone about me bringing her to your room if they don't ask. I really don't need this shit," I said as I clicked over to hear the long-awaited explanation.

"*Taj!!!! Taj!!!!*". I was hoping he didn't hang up. "Yeah, man, you kept me on hold so long that I damn near hung up. What's up?! What's the deal?!" Taj said, seeming so nonchalant. "She's dead, man," Taj hesitantly said. I hated telling him because he always sounded the least bit concerned about a woman's feelings. It's like he was born with an IDGAF bone in his body. This made me want to hang up in his face, but I needed the details of what happened. "Oh, sorry to hear that," he said and moved on in conversation as if we were casually talking about the football game.

I remember when Taj was messing with two females in the same unit. One was a private, and the other a captain. My boi was a fan of fucking up, not down. He always had a way with the woman and didn't care about rank; hell, neither did she, apparently. But when shit hit the fan and the captain became pregnant, she wanted more from him, even offering to move him to another unit so they could hide their relationship. He refused to leave because, honestly, he used her for the benefits that came from being under her tutelage. Plus, the female that he was really falling deeply in love with wasn't really easy on the eyes, but her body was built like she worked for a Fortune 500 company, a.k.a King of Diamonds, and could cook her ass off. She must've been reared by her grandparents, but I digress. Anywho, the Captain wanted him badly and threatened to say that she was raped if he didn't comply.

"Shit, no problem," he said. "Please tell them. My ring camera got you pulling up several times and sometimes unannounced, and Oh boy, the conversations we had outside were also picked up!!!! Please do it... I beg of you bitch".

Meanwhile, Shawty, who he was also seeing, had no idea. She just thought she was always riding him because she saw how eaten up he was as a soldier. Ha, the only thing that was eaten up, apparently, was her. All I know is she was a victim of a drive-by shooting and was pronounced DOA (Dead on Arrival) at the end of the story. And to this day, no one knows what happened to her. Of course, we all know that CID never solves shit, so until this day, it's an open case. I guess all is fair in love and war, or is it?! Look at me rambling. Let me get back to finding out what's happening with this nut.

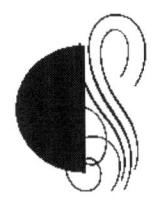

NEVER BITE THE HAND THAT FEEDS YOU

"OK, man, spill it.... what's the deal?!" I asked, anxiously awaiting his answer. "Well, you know....well, maybe you don't know, but Butler and I used to mess around, and she told me that she and ole boy from my last duty station, Fort Drum, were married. Do you remember me telling you about the ole boy they call Slope because his teeth were slanted? Well, I put that niggah on a game, and he turned his back on me in the middle of a deal...end of the story. Plus, that niggah owes me on a drop-off that came up short," Taj angrily said. "Man, was this some type of get-back?" I asked unsurprisingly. "Hell yeah! Now you know nobody wants Butler's ass; she thinks she's some type of City Girl or Meghan Thee Stallion. Done been with half the unit, and because she got a fat ass, she thinks she's owed a Birkin bag. *"Bitch please raise up off of these n.u.t's because you get none of these,"* he said jokingly in his Snoop Dog voice. "No, but seriously, that girl's for the streets. I was doing him a favor. I'm sorry she didn't make it. I was just being hospitable…. you know, the right thing to do," Taj said with a slight giggle. "No, the right thing would have been to leave her ass alone," I thought to myself.

"Water under the bridge, so what's next?" Taj said without hesitating. This has got to be the most heartless person in the world. "So, what is mean ass Dee up to? She still got that rope around yo balls?" he said as he laughed. He always tried to find humor in times of seriousness. I think that's his coping mechanism. Back in the day, when the teacher would go around the room and ask him to read, he would always try to act like he was choking or do something stupid because his ass couldn't read well. Honestly, he knew when his turn was coming like the rest of us. I personally used to count the number of people before me and then read the paragraph in advance to sound out the words I didn't quite know. On the other hand, Taj was so busy playing around that he fumbled almost every word he read, thus causing an uproar in the classroom. The teacher was so tired of his shit that she threatened to have him removed permanently. Honestly, I think his athletic ability kept him in that school. They always said athletes couldn't read; he was nothing short of proof. No one bothered to get him help because of his ability to make the school look good. Needless to say, stupidity has always been his go-to.

"Let me get off this phone, man; you are starting to piss me off," I said as I placed my finger on the dial tone. I don't know what the hell I'm gonna do, but I gotta do something to make sure that I clear my name if it comes up. The weekend is almost over, and all hell has broken loose around me. I can't wait until these results come back so I can move away from this foolishness.

(*RIIINNNGGG... RIIINNNGGG!!!!*) "Hey, I heard they found a dead body in the barracks at your unit!!!," said Dee. "Huh, what you said?! Who died?!" I asked as if I didn't know what the hell she was talking about. "Tasha called and told me that her friend Pam, who's friends with some specialist in the unit by the last name Harris, called and told her some girl was shot in the head and left for dead," a concerned Dee exclaimed. You see how people get shit twisted. Where in the hell did a gun come into play? I said to myself while scratching my head. The biggest concern is someone telling Dee I was there. Now, how in the hell did she find out? That is the bigger question. Either Dee knows and is playing me, or she is fishing for info. Either way, I ain't saying shit.

"So, did you hear about it or not?" she asked. "Umm, no, I haven't heard about that." Why am I lying about something that has nothing to do with me? "Let me call somebody and find out." My heart was pounding out of my chest. "How stupid of me," I thought to myself. "OK, call me back when you find out," she said. "Ok," I said without hesitance. Knowing good and well, I wasn't going to call her black ass back, but I'll say anything to get her off the phone…sheesh.

CANDYMAN

Driving back home, I could feel a pain in the pit of my stomach. It was a feeling that I had never felt before. Not only was Butler deceased, but I lied once again to my wife.... stupid, so fucking stupid!!!! This has absolutely nothing to do with me, I keep saying. Suddenly, I found myself staring out the window at a red light, waiting for the light to change. My mind drifted off, and all of a sudden, I was back at my aunt's house, lying in the bed in a fetal position. I saw a man entering my room with a towel wrapped around his waist. He pulled the cover from over my head. I was always scared growing up, so I always kept the cover over my head to keep the monsters away.

I'm only 8 years old. Yes, I still believe in monsters, and he was nothing short of one. As it plays on in my suppressed memory, it feels familiar to me, like this has happened before. "Aye... Aye, you up?" Says the masculine voice. I remember saying nothing because I didn't want my aunt to get mad at me. She felt like I had a vivid imagination anyway, and this was definitely something I wanted to forget. As I stated, I never said anything. He reached down in my pants and started fondling me. I was no stranger to his touch. My aunt left me with him often to work that God forsaken 3rd shift job she had, and Uncle Charles made use of the time that we had together.

At first, it was subtle... a massage on my shoulders, which then moved to a rub down my spine to my lower back. I would receive extra candy or maybe a toy if I acted right. Then, it was if you do this, I'll get you that. What kid doesn't like gifts? My aunt never thought anything about me sitting in his lap. He would always place me right where his dick was. It felt gross, but I thought this was supposed to happen. I mean, it never happened with my dad, but my dad wasn't as present in my life as Uncle Charles. I'm a child. I didn't know to tell my aunt that I could feel his dick getting hard as I sat between his legs.

He became familiar with my body. So, as my memory serves me, that night was nothing short of any other night he made himself familiar with me. After fondling me, he placed his dick up against my lips. I knew what was supposed to happen next. I was supposed to please him as I always did. This night, though, something happened; this night, he actually let go into my mouth. Usually, he would hold it in his hand as he was cumming, and I could see a thick, almost mucus texture seeping through his fingers. It looked disgusting. This particular night, I made a sound, a sound of disgust. I don't know if I was upset with myself or him. I could never tell anyone my first was my uncle. I would always say an older female babysitter took my virginity. It just sounded better when talking with the guys. At any rate, my aunt came home early. There were no ring cameras back then, so he was unaware of her arrival. She burst into the room, and Uncle Charles was standing in front of me, pulling his pants up. My aunt was no dummy; she knew what time it was. He came up with all these excuses, saying I pulled his pants down and then he was just showing me something. Needless to say, that was the end of Uncle Charles, who never married my aunt, so how was he my uncle?

I felt that this was my fault. I caused this. Now, I can't get any more presents from Uncle Charles, no more game playing. I always cause shit to happen, it seems. Dee seems to be the only thing that has happened right in my life. I just wonder why, all of a sudden, this memory came back. I hadn't thought about him since that day, or at least I tried not to. I never went to therapy; we just gave it over to the good Lord, per usual. It's the only way we do things in the black community. It's like water under the bridge, but it was a typhoon for me. Why is it so vividly coming to memory…why now?! I suppressed this for years, and I tried to block out everything from my childhood and move on with life as I knew it. "So, why now," I ask again?

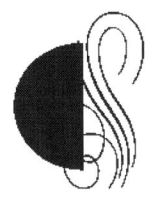

RUSSIAN ROULETTE

This feeling in the pit of my stomach I can not shake. I think I developed a conscience over the years, and it won't let me rest. It's like my world just closed in around me, and I'm the only one that noticed it. As I approached the gate, I realized I didn't have my ID card. I swear I would forget my head if it weren't attached to my shoulders. Damn, shoulder… shoulder, that's where I left it, in my jacket pocket in the backseat. I remember taking my jacket off after I left the store to pick up Items for the baby. This shit has to get better.

I pulled up to the gate and gave my ID to the SPC, who clearly wasn't paying any attention to what I handed him because he was so busy conversing with the other soldier in the shack with his feet plastered to the desk while leaning back in the chair. Usually, I would stop and correct him, but I can't; my mind won't allow me to be an overachiever today. "OK, you good?" said the scraggly-looking soldier as he handed me back my ID card, not once looking in my direction, and honestly, I'm glad he didn't. Plus, some of these new soldiers are so sensitive that I didn't want to risk the chance of seeing a stress card when I'm already stressed enough.

As I attempted to drive off, I heard someone call from the far right, "Aye, stop that car!!!". As I glanced over, I noticed that there was a random car check being conducted from the other security booth. Now, I'm at a standstill, and this niggah keeps staring at my car, and I ain't even on that side. I can see through my rearview that he is walking towards me with an armed security guard. "Pull over to the far left," he started saying as he waved his hands in a gesture to flag me down. As I pulled over to the left shoulder, the armed security guard stood still as the other tapped my window, signaling me to roll down my window. "Driver's License and proof of registration, please." "For what?! I was just checked, and no one said anything was wrong," I exclaimed to the officer. "Driver's license and proof of registration, please," he repeated. At this point, I'm becoming frustrated as I reach into the glove compartment to retrieve the requested items and hand them to him. "I stopped you because there is a large amount of blood in your backseat. Is everything OK? I noticed it as you were going through the line," said the officer. I glanced in the backseat, and as sure as shit stinks, there it was, plain as day. "Oh, no, officer, one of my friends hurt himself during a basketball game, and I forgot to clean up the blood. I just dropped him off at Grady to be checked out," I said nervously. Damn, I was quick on my feet with that one. "Oh, OK, well, make sure you clean that up; it almost looks like a murder scene," the officer said jokingly. I just laughed, knowing good, and damn well that's exactly what it was. "OK, be careful," he said as he backed away from the car, handing me back my items.

I slowly pulled back onto the road and up to the closest postal car wash center. I only had a dry towel and baby wipes that I had just purchased from the store. My dumb ass would pull up to one that no longer works, like every other thing on post. Here I am wiping up what looks to be a first 48-hour Crime, and who do I hear calling my name from the passenger side of somebody's car.... "Taj, that's who....this bitch ass niggah." I didn't even bother to look up.

"Man, what the hell are you doing?! You should have cleaned that dirty ass car a long time ago," he said while trying to be funny. I just continued wiping off my car's backseat as I moved from one side to the other, as though he said nothing at all. "So, what's the plan with 'ol girl? 'Ol boy home yet?" At this point, I looked up at him in disgust. "Bitch, don't ask me shit about that situation ...period. If you want to know something, ask someone else... I'm done," I said as I closed the door to my backseat and hopped in the driver's seat. I'm so pissed right now, and he would be the last person I want to see. I pulled off so fast that I damn near gave myself whiplash.

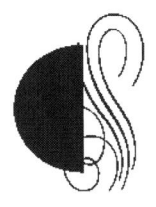

PUT ME IN THE GAME COACH

(*RIIINNNGGG…RIIINNNGGG!!!!*) "Yep," I answered. "I know yo ass collar popping and shit, but Tasha is at your house with Dee. She mentioned a girl dying at the unit. I told her I was on my way to check it out but needed to stop first. Anyways, I'm just letting you know," Taj said. I just hung up and proceeded to the house. Here are these thoughts again. My childhood traumas keep approaching me like an unwanted conversation from Taj. I now see myself standing in the shower after football practice. All of the other guys are gone except for Coach Ross, whom I started looking at like a father figure. He keeps saying, "If you don't hurry up, I'm going to come in there and turn that shower off." Coach Ross was always on the street raising money for uniforms to help out those who were less fortunate, and I just so happened to fall in that category. I think my aunt had a crush on him, and because he always spoke her language of God, she believed he was heaven-sent…knowing that the devil was also a fallen angel, but I digress.

I would go away to overnight travel games with him, and at first, it was OK because my boi Taj was there, but then he was kicked out of school, and his mom took him off the team. Now, I was left to fend for myself. It became awkward, however, the day that I was in the shower. I swear I turned the shower off when I heard his voice, but he came in anyway. "Man, what's taking you so long, ghost rider?! I hated that name, but for some odd reason, that was what he called me. Come on out of there; it's not like you got something that I haven't seen before," Coach said, acting as if he was trying to turn his head towards the lockers. At this point, I'm 13, and I've developed pubic hair in areas where only grown men should have hair. No one taught me anything about puberty. I mean, me and the guys talked about, I meant, lied about the girls we slept with. We even compared dick sizes, but we didn't know what the hell we were talking about.

I stepped out of the shower, but my towel was on the bench. "Can you throw me my towel, Coach?" I asked. "Man, come get this towel and put some clothes on so we could go," he replied. I walked out onto the cold, wet floor, with my feet slipping with every stride. As I approached the bench where my towel was lying, the coach picked the towel up and started striking at me as though we were playing a game. I was familiar with playing games. My Uncle Charles, or former Uncle Charles, always played this game with me. I commenced to laugh because I was nervous. What else was I to do?! I finally snatched the towel, and he allowed me to get dressed.

On the way to Taj's house (because my aunt was still working that 3rd shift job), Coach Ross turned to me and asked me what I knew about God. I told him I had only been to church twice, and they were both for my father's and my sister's funeral. "So, you don't know much about God, huh?!" "Nope. All I know is God is good, God is great, thank him for this plate. That was a ritual we went by before we ate," I said. We both laughed it off. Well, the bible also speaks of God being a forgiving God. "Do you know that he will forgive all of your sins?" he looked over in my direction and placed his hand on my knee. I turned my head out the window and proceeded to stare out into the open sky as though I was looking for an answer as to what to say next. "You're a good kid, Jac; I can see you going far in football; just allow me to guide you. I can see your name in lights and the crowd chanting SMITH!!! SMITH!!!!." "It would be nice to see bright lights instead of blue lights," I thought to myself briefly. That was before I was introduced to his hand moving further up my thigh towards my dick. "This can't be happening again," I thought to myself, but it did. He knew we were close to the house, so he pulled over into a vacant parking space and slid his hands down my pants. I was still flaccid, and by no means did I want to get excited. "You do want your name in lights?" he asked. "Yeah, I do, but not like this," "But what if this is the only way to get it?"

He then bent down to put his mouth on my dick. I never felt this feeling before. Uncle Charles always made me do that to him, and now I see why. It felt good. I hate myself and love my life at the same time. I remember a feeling coming over my body, and I couldn't control it. How come none of my friends ever talked about their uncle or coach? How come?! My body started to shiver, and I felt fluid leave my body like an out-of-body experience. He then pulled my pants up and proceeded to drive off like we had just ordered food from a fast-food restaurant. "How ya feeling, ghost rider?" he asked me as if this hadn't just happened. I responded with, "I'm OK." Hell, what else was I to say? I feel great?! Not even Tony the Tiger would have a comeback. "That's good, that's good," he responded. "I can see it now, you with all those fancy cars, fine women (notice he never said fine men), and lots of money."

We arrived at Taj's mom's house, and he let me out like nothing happened. He didn't even buy me anything to eat…ole niggah!!! "Remember, God forgives all sins, even the small ones," he said as I closed the door, "Remember God forgives ALL sins, even the small ones, he repeated. Just talk to him; he'll hear you." "Well, I didn't think he knew me because we had only met twice in my life, and since you know him so well, maybe you could talk to him for me." I just closed the door and rang the doorbell.

Ms. Green opened the door, let me in, and waved him off. She asked if I was okay, but I told her I was tired from practice. I took a shower and entered the room where Taj was sound asleep. I woke him up and told him about everything. He wanted to tell his mom immediately, but I told him it would ruin my chances of becoming a star. We swore one another to secrecy, and he promised not to say anything, and he never did. He's my brother…. my keeper.

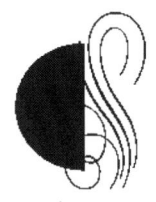

SAVE ME FROM MYSELF

This continued to happen to me for over a year, that is, until one of the other players had the courage to call him out for trying the same shit with him. I wish I was that brave, but who would listen to me? I guess I'm just a kid with a hell of an imagination. He was plastered all over the news and, of course, fired from his job. I don't know whether to say thank you, God, or no thank you because he's the same one that I met during both funeral services and again when I met Coach. I was at the lowest point in my life each time I met him. Yet, I was told to take ALL of my sins to him. What's a sin? Whatever it is, it must be something that's attached to me. Either way, I'm just grateful I no longer have to put up with that shit.

As I turned onto my street and parked in the driveway, I sat back for a minute. I needed to catch my breath and clear my thoughts on what had just happened. "That could have been my life behind bars in the blink of an eye," I thought to myself. I have a strong urge to roll up a blunt and forget all about the past few hours. Better yet, I'll just pop this Xanax I was prescribed down range. I just need something to take the edge off. I grabbed the half-drunken Sprite sitting in the cup holder, popped the top on the pill bottle, and chugged it down my throat as fast as possible. "Hurry up and kick in before I go in this house….please!!!!" I leaned my car seat back, turned the radio off, and closed my eyes just for a few seconds.

Before I knew it, Dee and our kids were knocking on the car window. Had 2 hours passed, and I did not know it?! (*Knock, Knock!!!!*). "I thought that I was about to collect them $400,000," Dee said as she stood there dangling our son off her hip and laughing. I crunk the car up and partially rolled the window down. "You just missed Tasha. She said the female that was shot in the head came from your unit, and guess what?! (I wish you could see the expression on my face). She said this girl was pregnant by somebody other than her husband." I opened the door to get out of my car, and lucky for her; my Xanax had already kicked in full speed ahead because all I heard was …..wonk wonk wonk wonk. I gotta get a refill of this shit.

"Did you get the items from the store?" Dee asked while opening the door and placing the baby in the rocker next to the sofa. "Oh shit, I knew it was something I forgot," I said. I ran back outside and grabbed the bag from the passenger side.

(*RIIINNNGGG…RIIINNNGGG!!!!*) "Hello!!!!" There was no response, so I hung up. (*RIIINNNGGG RIIINNNGGG!!!!*). Who's calling me from a blocked number?

"Aye, I don't have time to play on the phone. Who is this?!" I asked while feeling annoyed. "Yo, how are you doing, Big Sarge? This is Butler." "Butler as in male Butler, husband of the deceased female Butler?!!!" I thought to myself as my eyes got bigger. "Hey, what's up? I'm so sorry for your lost man," I said sympathetically. "How can I help you?" "Well. I'm trying to contact ya, boi Green. Do you have his number?" "Yeah, I got it, ummm, can I give you a call back in a few? I just got home, and I have some groceries in my hand." Now, I could have lied and said I didn't, but I'm unsure of what he wants, and he could have gotten the number from anyone, so why is he calling me?

I just walked back into the house, placed the bag on the table, and acted as though that call had never happened. Here goes Dee again, yapping about some damn sorority she's thinking about joining. "Hey, it's a military sorority/fraternity for anyone who joined the service, and I was thinking about joining. I think it's called Kappa Epsilon Psi, and the fraternity that will keep YOU busy is called Kappa Lambda Chi. I think that's the right name. Whatcha think? You can also tell Taj's selfish ass about it," she said. "OK, well, who told you about it?" I asked, acting as though I was interested.

"Lisa, Renee, and Atiya joined, and they loved it. You remember my crew back home, right?" I nodded and said, "Yep, as if I was still listening." I learned that was all I needed to do after I said my vows. "Well, Lisa told me that a group from the sorority called the DD214s get together and fellowship every week. It really helped her out." "I honestly would do anything to get out of this house," I thought to myself. "Ummm, well, I ain't joining no fraternity from the military," I said as I laughed. "I have better things to do with my time, but you can. Who's gonna watch these kids when you join because it's not guaranteed that Tasha will always be here." Honestly, I'm not feeding into this convo because what she doesn't know is that shit is about to hit the fan, and Tasha may be gone before you know it. "I don't know, I'll figure that out once I'm accepted," Dee said.

"The interest meeting is tonight at 1800 hrs. Will you be home?" She asked. "I think so. The results of the board should be back by Tuesday at the latest, fingers crossed," I said. "OK, great. Let me call and see if Joy and Shayla are going. It would be nice to be around familiar faces. I think Joy already joined a sorority, but it wouldn't hurt to ask," Dee said. I just nodded my head as if I was listening once again. In my mind, I'm thinking of anything to get her out of the house and out of my business.

Hours passed, and Dee left for her interest meeting, and of course, I had the kids. Not that I'm complaining, but after all the shit I went through these last couple of days, I could use a break, but the way this baby's lungs are set up, that won't be happening anytime soon. I've given him toys, food, and a bath, but all of that just seems to perpetuate this noise coming out of his mouth.

(*Hard knock at the door*). Now, who in the hell is at the door at this time of the day? I picked the baby up and walked towards the door while the others were watching television. Suddenly, I got an eerie feeling again in the pit of my stomach but proceeded to the door anyway. I looked out the peephole, and, once again, the tall, dark-skinned, slinky-ass man that was at my door before was back.

"How can I help you?" I asked. He moved his face closer to the peephole. Now we are eye to eye, as though he was trying to see inside my house…dumb ass. "Umm, is Taj here?" the man asked as he backed towards the steps. "Naw, he ain't here, he don't live here," I responded. "I said, is Taj here?" the man repeated as if he had never heard me the first time. Against my better judgment, I cracked the door open. Usually, I would have my piece on me, but I had a screaming baby in one arm while trying to get the door. But as soon as I cracked the door open, he ran towards me, kicked the door in, and pulled out his gun. I didn't know what to do. I pleaded for him not to shoot me or my kids. "He just kept asking, "Where is it?!" "Where is what?!". I asked because, at this point, I was confused, and all I could think about was my kids and Dee. He then directed me towards the backroom and forced me to sit down on the bed with my baby in my arms. It was as if my baby knew this man meant business, so he was as quiet as a church mouse. Where was this energy before I opened the door?!

The other two kids were standing in the doorway, screaming and crying hysterically. I begged them to go back and sit down and told them that it would be OK, but they could tell it wouldn't be. "Why are you here?" I asked while staring at the barrel of his gun. "Where is the black bag?" he demanded. "What fuckin black bag...I don't know what the hell you are talking about?" At this time, I can tell that he was serious about what he came for. "You can search the house, man, but I promise you I don't have anything here," I tried to explain. As he rummages through the drawers and tears up my closet, he pushes my son down. "Aye, you pushed my child, man; calm that shit, bro," I screamed. "Shut the fuck up before I shoot that lil niggah". By the way, he was staring at me; he was not playing. "I'm so glad Dee isn't here," I thought to myself.

"Get what you think you came for and leave, please, sir... please!!!! I don't have anything here!!!! It's just me and my kids," I exclaimed. He then taped me up and forced me into the closet while I was screaming, "Don't hurt my kids, please. Take whatever you want, but please don't hurt them." I guess he left the door ajar so that I could see what was taking place. Suddenly, I heard three loud gunshots, followed by dead silence. I tried to break away from the tape, but it was too tight. All I could do was scream...all I could do was scream, "No, No, No, please don't…what the fuck did you do?!" I could hear him leaving the room and heading down the hallway while opening every closet that led to the front door. He scurried out of the house, but I didn't hear a vehicle crank up. It's safe to say he's gone, but where are my babies? Please don't tell me that they're dead.

ALL ISN'T FAIR IN LOVE AND WAR

Hours passed, and finally, Dee made it home. "Aye, big head, guess what???? I had a great interview!!!! Why did you leave the door open again, fool?" she asked as she laughed. "Also, why is my house looking like this?! Jac, where are you?" She called my name several times as she approached the backroom. My biggest fear was what she would find once she stepped into what was once known as our sanctity. I could only tell she made it into the room by the way she let out a God-wrenching scream. "No God, No God..this can't be happening!!!" I called out to her so she would know I was still there but in the closet. She opened the door, and all I could see was blood splattered all over the wall in the room. "Who did this? Who the fuck did this,

Jac?!" she asked as she stood over me, pounding me in the back of my head with one hand while covered in blood from holding the lifeless body of our youngest son. The other two kids were deceased as well. One by the door, with her body positioned as though she was trying to run out of the room, and the other by the closet. I'm unsure if he was coming to rescue me, but he never made it. Damn!!!!

"I didn't do it, Dee. I swear I didn't do it," I squalled. "Cut me loose, please!!!!" She used her keys to cut through the tape that had me bound. I got up and immediately called 911 from her phone because this was a homicide that needed to be investigated.

After a short period of time, both CID and the local coroner showed up. I don't understand for the life of me why ole boy showed up at my home, but I knew for sure that Taj knew who this guy was. But I couldn't focus on that right now because my mind is all over the place. I am completely heartbroken. Watching our babies wrapped in white sheets and being loaded into the coroner's vehicle took me back to Iraq. I've seen so many dead bodies of both my battles and the Iraqis that it numbed me. I was always told I don't show emotions, but my childhood has a lot to do with this. I was always told to man up; little boys don't cry, faggots do, and all this was coming from a down-low man. Have you ever noticed that most people who criticize the sexuality of others, low key, want to be like them but are afraid of what others might think? That was both Uncle Charles and Coach....sorry ass niggahs.

Dee called Tasha for comfort, and Tasha was there in no time. The way she reacted to the death of the kids, you would have thought that they belonged to her. I was transported to the hospital to make sure I didn't sustain any more injuries while Dee and Tasha stayed behind. While I was questioned at the hospital, she had to go to the precinct for further investigation. I told them that it all happened quickly. I didn't know the man but had seen him before, and although I knew Taj knew him, I couldn't bring myself to put him in the mix, even after the passing of our kids. Why me? Why my home? It was like I was living the worst nightmare of my life.

The following week was all a blur. It came fast and went as fast as I could blink my eyes. The funeral service was more than one could take. Butler's death was still under investigation, and no service was set for her as of yet, but as stated, CID takes its time with some cases. That was not my concern at this moment. I just lost my kids, whereas she had just aborted hers and, as a result, lost her life. Imagine three kids lying in caskets before you. This was my first child, but Dee…my God Dee….she stood strong. Her faith in God was really tested, and she knew if she could get through this, she could make it through anything. She dressed them in both hot pink and blue. Jr. looked like he had just taken a nap, the kind you didn't want to wake him up from because you knew that once he was up, it was over. The only thing is that he was never going to get up again. They were never going to get up again.

Taj got up and stood alongside me, as did Tasha with Dee. Once I said my words of comfort and reflection, Taj followed suit; after all, he was the kid's Godfather.

During the repast, I couldn't eat. I just watched Dee go to every person and thank them for showing up as if they had just attended a wedding. How she did this with the kids just being buried was a mystery to me. This is why I love her so much. She is so vital when I find myself being weak. I looked around for my right-hand man, and he was nowhere to be found. This was too much for him, I'm sure. His mom, who was like an aunt to me, had just passed a year ago, and he hadn't seemed to get over that. If it ain't one thing, it's another, as some would say. All I ask is for God to give me strength that surpasses understanding.

Weeks after the kids were laid to rest, we received great news that the guy who broke into my home was apprehended. After a thorough investigation, we discovered that my neighbor across the street had a ring camera that picked up everything. It's amazing how far we've come with technology. Not only did the camera pick him up the day in question, but it also picked him up at 4 a.m., a couple of weeks prior, as he walked away from my home in the wee hours of the morning. Guess what?! It also picked up Taj waiting on the corner the day he broke in. I'm confused (scratching my head). "Why was Taj with him?" Come to find out after the investigation was complete that my boi, my brother, my ace, and my bestie set me up to be murdered. The morning the asshole came to the house, he chickened out, and because he was paid half up front, he had to finish the task at hand.

"I and Taj had been planning this move for a while now," he said. He informed the detectives that he received the first portion the day I saw them at McDonald's. Damn, that was the black bag he gave to ole boi. It makes perfect sense now, but still, why me? I always had his back, even before having my own. I put his family before mine, my career on the line several times for him, and this is how he repays me?! I pray you rot in hell niggah!!! Come to find out, Taj wanted me dead because he was jealous of the life I now had with Dee, and although he had everything he needed, he wanted more. After what seemed to be the worst time in our lives, I finally got that promotion I needed to take my family to the next level. I guess all isn't fair in love and war.

"You desire and do not have, so you murder. You covet and cannot obtain, so you fight and quarrel. You do not have, because you do not ask" James 4:2

Made in the USA
Columbia, SC
02 October 2024